Peppa's Christmas Wish

ISBN 978-0-545-56511-0

Published by arrangement with Entertainment One and Ladybird Books,

A Penguin Company.

All rights reserved. Published by Scholastic Inc.

SCHOLASTIC and associated logos are trademarks and/or registered trademarks of Scholastic Inc.

16 15 14 13 12

18 19 20 21 22/0

Printed in the U.S.A.   132
This edition first Scholastic printing, September 2013

This book is based on the TV series *Peppa Pig*
Peppa Pig is created by Neville Astley and Mark Baker

Peppa Pig © Astley Baker Davies Ltd/Entertainment One UK Ltd 2003.

www.peppapig.com

It is Christmas Eve, and Peppa, George, and their friends are aboard the Christmas Elf Train.

Toot, toot!

They are on their way to Santa's Workshop.
Everyone is very excited!

"Ho! Ho! Ho!" chuckles Santa Claus.
"I hope you've all been good!"
He makes a list of what everyone would
like for Christmas.

George would like a racing car.
Peppa would like a doll.

Peppa and her family are spending Christmas with Granny and Grandpa Pig.
"You can stir the Christmas pudding," Granny Pig says. "And don't forget to make a wish!"

Soon it is bedtime.

"I hope Santa knows where Granny and Grandpa Pig live," Peppa whispers before she falls asleep.

On Christmas Day, Peppa and her family
eat the Christmas pudding.
"This is delicious!" snorts Mummy Pig.
"I wonder what you wished for when
you were making it, Peppa."

It is time to open presents.
George got a racing car.

Vroom! Vroom!

But there is nothing under the tree for Peppa.
"Santa has forgotten me," Peppa says sadly.

Santa is on his way home in his sleigh. Suddenly, he spots something at the bottom of his sack.

"Oh, ho, ho!" Santa gasps.
"There is one last present to deliver!"

Santa tumbles down the chimney
at Granny and Grandpa Pig's house. "Here's
your present, Peppa!" He chuckles.
"My Christmas pudding wish came true!"
Peppa cries. "I wished that Santa would
visit us on Christmas Day, and he has!"
Hooray for Santa!

Snowy Fun!

Peppa and George are excited today
because it's snowing!
"Can we go outside?" asks Peppa.
"Yes," replies Mummy Pig,
"but you must bundle up first."

The two little piggies put on their warm,
wooly clothes and run out into the snow.
"Come on, George!" calls Peppa.
"Let's make footprints!"

Splat! Peppa runs so fast, she falls over
and lands headfirst in the snow!
"Hee, hee, hee!" laughs George.
"It's not funny!" Peppa says.

"George!" cries Peppa. "Let's make snowballs!"
Peppa picks up some snow,
tosses it at George, and laughs.
George giggles, too. He wants to make a
snowball just like Peppa.

After they're done playing, Peppa has an idea.
"Let's build a snowman!" she says.
Peppa and George roll up large balls of snow.
Then they find sticks for the snowman's arms,
and stones for his eyes and mouth.

Next, Peppa makes the snowman's nose
with a big orange carrot.
"He needs clothes to keep him warm," says Peppa.
George runs inside to find some wooly clothes.
The snowman is very happy!

Mummy and Daddy Pig come outside.
Mummy is wearing her warm, wooly clothes, but
Daddy looks cold and grumpy.
"I don't know where my winter clothes are,"
says Daddy.
"I think I know." Mummy Pig smiles.

Daddy Pig's hat, scarf, and gloves are
all on the snowman, of course!
Peppa, George, Mummy, and Daddy Pig laugh
so much, they fall over in the snow.
What a fun winter day it has been!